MARY ELLEN

By May Justus

First published in 1947

An early version of this story was published

under the title *Near-Side-and-Far* in 1936.

This unabridged version has updated grammar and spelling.

© 2019 Jenny Phillips

www.thegoodandthebeautiful.com

Illustrated by Marybelle Kimball

Cover illustration by Ecaterina Leascenco

Cover design by Phillip Colhouer

To Rosalind
who is an old friend of Mary Ellen's

Author's Acknowledgment

The author wishes to thank James Watt Raine
and Mellinger Henry for the music of
folk songs used in this book.

Table of Contents

1
The Trip over Big Log Mountain

The preacher man, Brother Martin, brought Granny Allen's message to the Morrison family.

She was tired of living all by herself on Near-Side of the mountain and wanted one of the Morrison children to come and stay with her through the winter.

There was great excitement over this announcement. There were seven of the Morrison children—but which one of them could be spared was a very difficult question. Not big Abe, who was nearly grown and a right-hand man to Father, whom he helped in the work. Not Ike and Jake, who were twins and could never be parted. Not Dilly, who was to be married at Christmas and who was busy making coverlets and feather beds for her new home across the mountain. Cissie was only five years old and would be of no help to Granny, and Tom Tad certainly belonged in no other place but his cradle.

"I reckon it will have to be Mary Ellen," Father said. "It will come mighty hard to spare her, but she's not too young, and she's not too old to suit Granny."

Mary Ellen came in the middle of the family and was ten years old—ten and going on eleven, as she always added when telling her age.

She had never been away from home in her life, never been to Granny Allen's on Near-Side. All the world she knew was Far-Side of Big Log Mountain. Here she went to school four or five months a year, and to Big Meeting when the preacher man came to preach. But she knew the world was bigger.

Granny Allen made several trips a year during the good weather and spoke of the people and places on Near-Side of Big Log Mountain. It was called Near-Side because it was nearer to Crossville, the railroad station, than Far-Side, which was many mountain miles away.

"Yes, I reckon we'll have to let Mary Ellen go," said her mother, and she said it rather sadly, for she loved all seven of her brood, and one as much as another.

"It will be a good chance for her to go to school," the preacher man told them. "The school here will close around Thanksgiving, but the Mission school lasts all winter."

Mary Ellen's heart beat high with joy.

"Is that a school with glass windows?" She had heard Granny Allen speak of this school. She always called it the Mission. She sold eggs to the schoolteacher there, and sometimes huckleberries.

Brother Martin nodded. "It's a fine school. Miss Ellison's a 'brought-on-teacher' and a 'doctor-woman' all in one. I've heard her make speeches—pretty nigh as good as a preacher man herself. And all of Near-Side yonder goes to the Mission for toothache drops or if a body gets rattlesnake bitten."

Mary Ellen thought of something else.

"Can you see the train from Granny Allen's?"

Granny had spoken of the train which stopped at Crossville, the nearest railroad station for the people who lived on Big Log Mountain.

"Well—" the preacher man hesitated, as if he were trying to be certain, "I'm not plumb certain-sure about it. It's a good way from Granny Allen's. But you can see the smoke all right, when it's not too cloudy, and hear the engine whistle, too."

This was enough for Mary Ellen. She had lived here on Far-Side all her life. She had never crossed over the mountain to Near-Side where Granny lived. And now she was going! Tomorrow! How happy, how excited she was!

Everybody helped her to get ready. Mother washed and ironed the blue gingham dress and starched the white sun-bonnet. Father got out the last and resoled the shoes. Ike and Jake made a pair of strings from a piece of groundhog hide they had tanned.

"They'll never break on you," they assured her.

Big Abe tuned up his banjo that night and played all his ballad songs for her. He played "Lonesome Dove" twice because it was her favorite.

"Down in some lonesome piney grove,
Down in some lonesome piney grove,
Down in some lonesome piney grove,
A little dove tells of her love."

Mary Ellen sang it from memory. She had learned it from her mother, who always sang when she was at work.

Dilly fried chicken for breakfast next morning and made three pans of biscuits so that there would be plenty for a lunch to pack in the saddlebags later.

It was early in October, and pleasant weather, but the air was chill that morning, and Mother put a little hood on Mary Ellen's head before she put on the sunbonnet. She put two hot potatoes in her coat pockets so that she might curl her fingers around them and keep warm.

They gathered on the porch to see Brother Martin and Mary Ellen start up the mountain.

"Be a good child, honey," Mother said. "Be all the help you can to Granny."

Mary Ellen looked back to wave.

"Get your head full of sense," advised Father.

"So you can divide with us!" said big Abe, who had never taken to schooling but was very proud of Mary Ellen's book learning.

"Don't get stuck-up," warned one twin.

"Or biggety," added the other.

Mary Ellen knew they were only joking, so she laughed and made no answer.

Cissie waved once, then hid her face in the fold of her mother's apron.

"Goodbye! We got to mosey along," Brother Martin told them. Then he turned the horse's head toward the trail. "Get along—get along, Gospel."

Mary Ellen, perched on Gospel's back behind the preacher man, looked back to wave at the turn of the trail. Then they started up the mountain, and she had to turn around and hold on tight. The chill of the early morning disappeared as the sun rose. A thin gray mist from the hollow softened the rugged mountainside and hid the way before them until they were halfway to the top.

Brother Martin raised a tune. "I'm in the habit of singing, and now I can't help it," he told Mary Ellen. "Singing is good company and comfort, too."

Perhaps he thought that Mary Ellen was feeling rather lonesome just then and needed a tonic to cheer her up. He went on with the song:

"I am bound for the promised land,
I am bound for the promised land,
O, who will come and go with me?
I am bound for the promised land."

The tune of this old hymn was so joyful that Mary Ellen's spirits rose with it, and she joined her voice with the preacher man's in the next refrain.

And now they had reached the top of the mountain. How beautiful the other side before them was, with flashes of reddening sumac and sourwood among the dark green of the pines.

How far it seemed to the foot of the mountain where a little valley curled like an uneven ruffle on a big green apron.

"Is this Near-Side?" asked Mary Ellen.

"Near-Side it is," Brother Martin told her. "And if you squint your eyes and look down there, you can see the smoke from somebody's chimney."

Mary Ellen squinted and looked where he pointed with his finger. Yes, she *could* see a little gray wisp of smoke. Perhaps somebody was getting dinner. It was dinner time. The morning sun had traveled with them over the mountain and now looked down through the tops of the pines. Mary Ellen was feeling hungry and thought of the lunch in the saddlebags. She wished that the preacher man would think a little bit about it, too. But he was singing another meetinghouse hymn:

"We shall rest in the fair and happy land,
Just across from the evergreen shore."

Mary Ellen liked this song. Mother often sang it
while she went about her work in the home or rocked
Tom Tad in his cradle with her foot upon the rocker
while her hands were busy with her knitting.

"We shall rest in the fair and happy land." Mary
Ellen found herself singing the song with the preacher
man. They sang as they went down the mountainside.
The trail made a big turn around a spur and dropped
into a little hollow. Brother Martin halted his horse.

"This is Indian Spring," he told her. "Best water on
the mountain. I reckon we'll stop here for dinner."

This was welcome news to Mary Ellen. She slid
from the back of old Gospel and ran to look into the
rocky bowl where the clear cold water bubbled and
ran out into a pebbly creek.

Mary Ellen took off her sunbonnet and hung it on a
nearby limb. Then she washed her face over and over
till she felt delightfully fresh and cool. By this time the
preacher man had taken the bundle of lunch from his
saddlebags, and Mary Ellen spread it on a flat rock.

"Dinner is ready," she said, just as Mother would
have done. Then she had a sudden recollection.

"Return thanks, Brother Martin."

He bared his head. "Let's sing 'Praise God' from *Old
Hundred* for the blessing." And they sang it together. It
sounded clear and beautiful in the still midday woods:

"Praise God, from whom all blessings flow;
Praise Him, all creatures here below;
Praise Him above, ye heavenly host;
Praise Father, Son, and Holy Ghost.

Amen."

Immediately after the amen, Mary Ellen passed the chicken, the brown biscuits, and the stack cake put together with huckleberry jam. She took nothing till the preacher man had taken all that he could manage, for this would have been very impolite. Mary Ellen was a civil-minded child, as she had overheard a neighbor woman say, and she tried to live up to her reputation.

How good everything was that day! Each bite seemed better and better.

The preacher man said it was the long ride that made them both so hungry. Mary Ellen was certain that the food had a much finer flavor than food ever had at home.

After their dinner was over, they had another drink from the spring. Then the preacher man hunted up old Gospel, who had been loosed for a little while to pick his own dinner.

Soon they were on their way again.

A part of the trail they traveled that afternoon was very difficult, being both steep and rocky, so that they had to go carefully. Old Gospel occasionally stumbled in the roughest places. Halfway down the mountain, the trail turned into a creek bed, rougher still, but not so steep. After a while, a turning led up a cove.

"No-End Hollow," said the preacher man.

"No-End? But where does it go?" queried Mary Ellen, who could not see very far ahead on account of Brother Martin's shoulders.

He laughed. "Well, it just keeps going on and on around the mountain till it runs into itself again."

"Oh, I see," said Mary Ellen.

After a while, they made another turn. Again they seemed to be climbing.

"Oh, I thought we went *down* the rest of the way," exclaimed Mary Ellen.

"This is Piney Spur," said the preacher man. "It's sort of like a knot on a log, up and down together. We'll be at Granny Allen's soon, just as soon as we round the point."

The point was the summit of the ridge. On the other side was a small clearing, and in the middle was a gray log house—two rooms with a porch between them. In this porch, called a dog-trot, sat Granny Allen peeling pumpkin and hanging the big yellow rings on a pole to dry.

She saw her visitors and rose.

"Howdy, Brother Martin! How you come on? God love ye, Mary Ellen!"

She shook hands with the preacher man, hugged
and kissed Mary Ellen, and offered them a drink
from the gourd dipper which stood in the cedar
water piggin.

"Sit down and make yourselves at home," was
her kind invitation as she brought out a rocker for
the preacher man and a little stool for Mary Ellen.
But Mary Ellen was tired of sitting down. She stood
on one foot, then the other, wishing she could run
around a bit. Granny Allen guessed her feelings.

"Saunter around if ye've got a mind to do so, Mary
Ellen. Piddle about the place as ye please and get
acquainted with it."

Mary Ellen skipped away. She ran around the
corner of the cabin and found a little path which led
to a spring. Over it was built a spring house. It would
be nice for wading in hot weather. Near the spring
was an empty water piggin. She filled it and carried it
back to the house. It eased the little lonesome feeling
to do a homey task like this. Then she went out to pick
up kindling, taking a basket she found by the hearth.
She wasn't wearing an apron, and the blue gingham
must be kept nice for go-to-meeting wear on Sunday.

When she came back with the basket so full of
chips that it was spilling, Granny met her at the door.
The preacher man had departed, and the evening fire
had been kindled on the hearth.

"Well, honey, have you earned your supper! Spry as a bug you be. I can see you take after your granny!"

Her laugh cackled out. Mary Ellen laughed, too. The fire on the hearth burned brighter.

"Bar the door for the night," said Granny, "and we'll both get supper."

2

Mary Ellen Sits by a Window

The first day at the Mission school, Mary Ellen did very little but look in wonder all about her at all there was to see.

The schoolhouse itself was a sight to behold, twice as big as the one on Far-Side, and just as she had always heard, it had glass windows! The only windows she had ever seen before were openings with shutters, which let in the wind as well as the sun and had to be closed in stormy weather. She was very glad, indeed, to be given a seat quite close to a window that framed a picture of Piney Point and a gap far down the valley where the train passed through twice a day. The turn on the spur of the mountain hid the train itself from view, but one could hear the engine's whistle and see its smoke curling up against the sky, a beautiful sight and thrilling.

The schoolroom was a beautiful place. Mary Ellen liked the pictures that hung on the walls. One reminded Mary Ellen of her own mother with Tom Tad. Under it was a word: *Madonna*. There was one of Abraham Lincoln, and another called *The Good Shepherd*.

She was very glad to be given a seat quite close to a window.

Miss Ellison was a picture herself as she sat behind a table on which stood a vase of blue gentians that matched the dress she was wearing.

Each pupil had a desk. The top was smooth and shiny like a new chestnut just out of the burr. On Far-Side of Big Log Mountain, there had been no desks—just benches long enough to hold half a dozen children. No place to put one's books at all, and so they were always spilling on the floor with a flutter and flop.

In the seat behind her sat Lovie Lane, who showed her all the lessons and explained whatever she needed to know. She was just about the age of Mary Ellen, and the two became good friends right away. Before recess that morning, they had exchanged tokens of their friendship. Mary Ellen gave Lovie a chinquapin bracelet in return for a set of picture postcards, and Lovie added a pressed wildflower to show her generous feeling.

At recess when the teacher gathered the children to play games in the schoolyard, Mary Ellen hung back, feeling suddenly shy among all the strange faces.

"What shall we play?" Miss Ellison asked. There was a chorus of voices:

"The Farmer in the Dell!"

"No—Ring-Around-the-Rosy!"

"London Bridge!"

"Have You Seen My Sheep!"

Miss Ellison considered a minute, as if she were

trying her best to decide. Then she noticed Mary Ellen standing alone against a big pine tree, watching the other children.

"Come, Mary Ellen, you haven't voted on which game to play," said the teacher.

Mary Ellen blushed and looked down at her toes.

"I never heard of those games," she answered. "We never played any of those on Far-Side."

"They are all nice games," said the teacher, "and easy to learn, as you will see." Then she turned to the other children. "Let's let Mary Ellen choose the game we shall play this morning. Then she may learn to play it with us."

Everyone thought this was a good idea. So Mary Ellen chose London Bridge because, at that minute, it was the only new game that she could remember.

She and Lovie Lane made the bridge by standing face to face with each other and holding hands as high as they could. The other children passed under in a long line, singing these words:

> "London Bridge is falling down, falling
> down, falling down,
> London Bridge is falling down,
> My fair lady!"

There were more verses to the song, more than Mary Ellen could remember, but she learned the tune in no time at all and managed to keep up with Lovie. In the end, there was a tug of war, a great deal of excitement, and much fun when the line broke and everybody tumbled.

"I like that game," said Mary Ellen. "I believe that I like it better than Miley Bright."

"That's a new game to us—to me, at least," said the teacher. "Will you show us how to play it, Mary Ellen?"

"Oh, yes!" was the ready answer. But just then the bell had to be rung, and playtime was over until dinner.

Mary Ellen went back into the schoolhouse a much happier person. The faces about her looked friendlier. A comfortable sense of belonging filled her heart as she settled in her seat and took out her book to study.

When the lessons were over in the afternoon, Miss Ellison read them a story, and Mary Ellen pricked up her ears. *Robinson Crusoe!* Why, there was a piece about him in one of her readers. But Miss Ellison was reading something else, a brand-new story. She had always wanted to know what happened to Crusoe and his man, Friday. Now, if she listened, she might find out! It was a most interesting story. Mary Ellen wished it would go on and on. Crusoe and Friday were having one adventure after another.

But the teacher looked at the little gold watch she

had taken from her pocket two times before that afternoon.

Four o'clock. Time to go home. The sun had dipped behind the Point. The shadows were stealing up from the gap. Everybody ran to get wraps and mittens. Although it was still October, there was a tingle in the air that foretold Jack Frost's coming.

"Button up tight," the teacher said to the circle of little children who gathered around her to say goodbye as they made themselves ready. She gave a helping hand to some of them, and Mary Ellen lent her assistance to one or two who had no older brother or sister. That is how it happened that she was left alone with the teacher when the others had departed. Miss Ellison saw her looking at something that was on her table. It was the *Robinson Crusoe* book. She was much too shy to touch it, though she longed to get her fingers on it, to open its enchanting pages, to gaze upon the colorful pictures inside.

"Do you like to read?" the teacher asked.

"Oh, yes!" The words came in a hurry. "I do—I do! I've read all my readers a dozen or more times over."

"And the other books—storybooks like *Robinson Crusoe?*"

"I guess I'd like a storybook right well."

It wouldn't be mannerly, she was thinking, to say she had never read a storybook, or to hint that she would like this one.

But Miss Ellison knew many things besides long

division and the proper way to pronounce hard words. She gave the book to Mary Ellen.

"Take Mr. Crusoe along with you," she said. "He'll be good company for you on the way home. I have two copies. Keep this one as long as you like."

"Oh!" Mary Ellen's eyes were shining. "Then I can read it all for myself—I'll read it aloud to Granny."

Then she said goodbye and hurried home. If the trail was steep, she didn't mind it. If she stumbled now and then, she never noticed it. She held the treasure folded safely against her heart, thinking all the way of the pleasure in store for her and Granny that night. She thought with growing satisfaction of the big pile of pine knots in the chimney corner. She was glad she had helped Granny gather a lot of them the day before. There would be a good light for reading.

Granny met her at the door.

"Well, Honey, come in and tell me how you made out the first day!"

Mary Ellen was quite willing. She was eager to tell of that day's adventure, but how to begin, where to begin? Well, she must start her story! And this is how she started it:

"Oh, Granny, I sit by a window!"

It was a lengthy tale. It lasted till suppertime and after. So many happy things had happened that day!

3
The Fun at a Quilting Bee

One day Lovie Lane brought a piece of news to school: her mother was to have a quilting bee the following Saturday! Granny Allen, who was considered a master hand at quilting, was invited to come, and so, of course, was Mary Ellen.

Lovie took Mary Ellen off to herself when she got to school that morning and told all of this in one breath. She was happy to think that Mary Ellen was to visit her a whole day.

"We'll have us a time!" she promised. "We'll crack hickory nuts and popcorn, and maybe make molasses candy."

"Are any other children coming?" Mary Ellen asked.

"I reckon so!" Lovie answered. "Mammy has asked all the neighbor women, and some of them have nine or ten children. Aunt Polly Pennybacker has thirteen, counting the littlest baby. We'll have us a time—a big time!"

Next day she brought news about the dinner they were going to have at the party. There was to be a host of good things. Lovie counted them off on her fingers: chicken pot pie, crackling bread, muscadine preserves, and stack cake. She had to stop and tell all about the stack cake.

"A sight to behold!" said Lovie. "The biggest cake you ever saw—seven layers high, with huckleberry jam for filling!"

Mary Ellen could imagine how that cake looked. She could almost imagine how it tasted. Then Lovie put her hand in her pocket and said, "Guess what I brought you for a present!"

Mary Ellen looked surprised. "Oh—I don't know!"

"I reckon you don't!" laughed Lovie. "But guess anyway."

"Persimmons, then."

"No, guess again."

"Maybe chestnuts."

"Wrong twice."

"A piece of store-bought candy?"

"Wrong three times! It's an eggshell cake." And she gave it to Mary Ellen.

"Oh, how pretty!" Mary Ellen exclaimed. It might have been a cake for a hummingbird, so very light and tiny it was, baked in the half of an eggshell.

"It's just a bite," said Lovie to her friend, "but a mighty good bite, I reckon. Mammy always bakes a little eggshell cake out of what sticks to the bowl."

"And you brought it to me! How good are you, Lovie!"

"Oh, I got to lick the spoon!" said Lovie.

That was on Friday, and the next day was to be the quilting party.

Mary Ellen and Granny rose early that Saturday morning in order to get a good start.

"For I hate to be late to anything," Granny Allen said, "no matter what, a party or a burying. If I go, I want to be on time."

Mary Ellen didn't mind how fast Granny hurried. She hurried, too. She hung the kettle on the crane and set the oven on a bed of coals to heat for baking the bread. While Granny milked, Mary Ellen fed the chickens after she had heated their corn, for this was Granny's recipe to make hens lay in cold weather.

Granny and Mary Ellen ate their breakfast close to the fire, for it was a chilly morning. How good the hot corn dodgers were, and the curly crisp bacon and gravy.

It didn't take long to wash the dishes, to bank the fire with ashes, and to latch the door. Then they were off!

At the Lanes' house, they found they were the first to arrive at the quilting party.

"I'm glad you're early," Lovie said. "We can have a lot of fun together before any of the others come." And she smiled at Mary Ellen.

They all went to look at the quilt, which swung in its frame from the ceiling.

"A Love Apple quilt!" exclaimed Granny Allen. "And as pretty as a picture."

Mary Ellen thought it was pretty, too.

"But don't the little red apples look a lot like tomatoes?" she asked.

"They do," agreed Granny. "And that is just what they are. My old grandmother told me that when she was a little girl, people thought tomatoes were poison and grew them in their flower beds because they were so pretty. Boys would take bouquets of them to their sweethearts when they went a-courting, and that's how they got the name 'love apples.'"

Everybody enjoyed the story, and Lovie Lane's mother laughed and said, "Granny Allen, you're a fair-witted woman. I never heard that tale afore myself!"

Then Lovie and Mary Ellen ran out to be by themselves a while. Lovie showed her friend the good things for dinner on the kitchen table. She let her peep at the stack cake in the cupboard. Then they went down the creek to a place which Lovie called the persimmon orchard, a thicket of persimmon trees, laden with their frosty yellow fruit.

The persimmons on the ground were much sweeter than those which they shook from the branches, and the wrinkled, dried-up looking ones were the very best of all.

While they were basking like lizards in the sun, they heard a halloo up the hollow, and Lovie answered, making a trumpet of her hands.

Another whoop, and then a pack of children and dogs bore down upon them.

"Aunt Polly Pennybacker's set," said Lovie, "and some others. Now we shall have fun."

Mary Ellen saw some familiar faces—children who went to the Mission school. Others she had never seen. But she didn't feel at all shy. Everybody was out to have a big time, and everybody seemed good-natured. They played games all that morning in the woods, choosing spots in the sun. The favorite game was Whoopee Hide—the name for Hide-and-Seek in the mountains—and another they liked almost as well was "What Time O' Day?"

No wonder they were all glad to run to the house when the hunting horn sent the call for dinner.

The quilters had already eaten and were back at work again. Lovie's mother was washing dishes and setting the children's table when they got to the house. Lovie helped, and so did Mary Ellen. There were not enough dishes to go around, so Lovie and Mary Ellen agreed to wait on the other children and to eat last of all.

Mary Ellen was willing to do this, but she couldn't help wondering whether they would have anything to eat when everybody else was done. The pot pie disappeared in a hurry. The muscadine preserves soon

The best part of the fun was pulling the candy.

vanished. The next-to-the-baby little Pennybacker boy demanded the very last crumb of the stack cake. Mary Ellen's hopes sank. But Lovie smiled across the table, and Mary Ellen smiled back. She would never let on that she was hungry or minded missing her dinner.

When the others finished dinner, Lovie sent them out to play.

"Mary Ellen and I will eat a bite and wash up the dishes," she said.

"I'll show you a surprise," Lovie said. She went to the old corner cupboard and brought back a platter heaped with everything from chicken pot pie to stack cake with huckleberry jam!

That afternoon the children popped corn, using for a popper an old-fashioned, three-legged skillet with a tight-fitting lid. They made molasses candy, too, as Lovie had promised Mary Ellen, and everybody got sweetened inside and out. The best part of the fun was pulling the candy into long yellow strings which could be twisted or braided and made into all sorts of curious shapes. Everybody had some to take home to help remember the happy occasion.

"I like a quilting party," remarked Mary Ellen to Granny. They were climbing the trail toward home in the late afternoon.

"Well, so do I," said Granny Allen. "There's more than one reason that makes a quilting party a whole passel of fun."

4

How Granny Got the Prize

Mary Ellen came skipping up the trail one afternoon and dashed through the cabin doorway in a manner that startled Granny Allen, who was settled down to quilt-piecing.

"Mercy me, child!" she exclaimed. "You seem mighty much in a hurry. You pretty nigh scared me out of my skin!"

Granny Allen peered over her spectacles and bent her sharp eyes upon her granddaughter.

Mary Ellen laughed. "I am in a hurry, Granny—in a big hurry to tell you some news. There's a big fair on Friday at the Mission in Forked Branch, and the whole school is going. The teacher is going around and getting the men to promise wagons. Oh, Granny, may I go, too?"

Granny smiled at the eager face and paused in matching a square.

"Seems as if you might do so," she replied. "I see no hindrance at all."

"Oh, Granny!" The little girl clapped her hands and spun around on a toe till her blue gingham skirt spread out like a morning glory. "Oh, Granny! What fun it will be. I've never been that far away from home—it's all of ten miles away—and there will be so much to see. The teacher wants us all to go. She says it will be very ed-ed-u-cational."

Granny Allen nodded her head. She was not sure about the meaning of the word, but whatever the schoolteacher said must be true, of course.

"No doubt," she agreed. "I am glad for you to go. And I'll sell the black hen's setting of eggs and buy you new cloth for a dress."

"Oh, Granny, you are so good to me!" Mary Ellen gave her a hug, and then she slipped outside. She was so full of joy that day that she had to dance all about the place.

The next afternoon when Mary Ellen came home, it was Granny who had a piece of news, and it, too, was about the big fair.

"The preacher man came by today and read me a piece about the fair. They are giving a lot of prizes away—mostly money prizes, too. I can't call 'em all to mind now. But the one I do remember is a prize that's offered for the prettiest patchwork quilt made by a woman over sixty years of age—" Granny paused in the telling of her tale and regarded her work spread over her lap and overflowing on the clean floor.

"If I could get this done in time, I'd like to send it in," she said. "This wild rose pattern takes everybody's eye—and it might have a right likely chance."

"It's the prettiest quilt you've ever made, Granny!" said Mary Ellen as she traced the lovely pink petals stitched on a square. "Granny, do send it to the fair."

"I've a mind to do that," Granny said, "if I get it done in time," she added. "I lack several squares. And I've got to take some time to finish your dress, too. It's partly cut out there on the bed."

Mary Ellen ran to see. "Oh, a *pink* dress, Granny!" she cried. "And I've wanted a pink dress for such a long time. It's the color of a rose—a wild rose, Granny, the same as your wild rose quilt."

"Just the same," agreed Granny. "I thought you'd like that, and it matches the roses in your cheeks."

Mary Ellen blushed at these words until the roses that blossomed in her plump little face were brighter than those in the patchwork quilt.

When Mary Ellen arrived home from the Mission school the next day, Granny Allen was working on her dress. The skirt and waist were done, but there was no cloth for collar and sleeves.

"The price of eggs is low again," said Granny. "That's why I didn't get enough—and it takes a half yard more for a dress for you than it did last year."

She studied a moment with wrinkled brow. "I'll just have to do it," she said as if she were thinking out loud. "There is no other way. I'll have to use the piece of cloth I saved to make the other squares."

She went to her work-bag and got a roll of pink. She had spread it out on the bed and had started the scissors along a fold before Mary Ellen realized just what Granny meant to do. Granny was giving her the cloth she had saved to finish her quilt—she was giving it to make the new dress. Oh, that must never be!

"Stop, stop, Granny!" she exclaimed.

Granny dropped the scissors to the floor with a clatter.

"What ails you, child?" she asked.

"Oh, Granny, you must finish your quilt—you must send it to the fair! Please use the new cloth for that—I can wait a while for the dress. I can wear one of my old ones."

"I meant to send the quilt," Granny said, "but it might not get a prize anyway—and I know you want a new dress."

"No, I don't, Granny—not now," said the girl. "I would rather take your quilt to the fair."

She persuaded Granny to listen to her, so the patchwork quilt was finished, and the new pink dress was put away to be finished later on when they should be able to buy more cloth.

It was fun the next morning to climb into the wagon, which had stopped in front of their home, and take her place with some more children, all off to see the big fair. Mary Ellen was scrubbed as fresh and clean as soap and water could make her. The old blue gingham dress was clean, too. What if it was faded a bit? Did she not have across her lap a carefully wrapped bundle—Granny's precious wild-rose patchwork quilt?

Oh, that long trip—she would never forget it. At last, they arrived at the Mission school where the fair was held. The school at Forked Branch was such a big one, so much bigger than their own school. There was so much to see. But before Mary Ellen would start out sightseeing, she sought Miss Ellison, her schoolteacher, and told her about Granny's quilt.

"I'll take charge of it," the teacher said. Then Mary Ellen scampered off to see what was to be seen. It took quite a time to make the rounds. There was really a lot to see: fruits and vegetables exhibited in beautiful and orderly array; rugs and woven coverlets; patchwork spreads—Mary Ellen's eye caught the sight of a quilt which she recognized as Granny's.

"What's that blue string pinned on it for?"

"That's the prize quilt," somebody said.

Mary Ellen's heart seemed to stop.

"But I thought the prize was money," she gasped.

Several who were standing by laughed, and Mary Ellen felt ashamed. She must have made a foolish remark, and she felt her face flush red.

But the schoolteacher came up just then.

"Granny's quilt won the ribbon," she said. "That's pinned on it to show it has won the prize. Oh, Mary

Ellen, won't you be glad to take it back to her—
five dollars!"

"Oh, yes!"

It was all she could say. Five dollars! They had
never had that much money all at one time before.
Oh, wouldn't Granny be happy over it! It seemed to
the little girl that she could hardly wait to put the
prize money in Granny's hand.

Turning to the teacher, she exclaimed, "Oh, I feel as
if I couldn't keep the good news from Granny. Is it a
very long time till we start back home?"

Miss Ellison smiled down at her.

"Not very long," she answered. "In fact, I think we'll
hurry a bit. Good news shouldn't wait too long."

"Granny's quilt won the ribbon!"

5

Pair of New Shoes

Mary Ellen stood in the square of sunlight that fell across the floor of the cabin and regarded the toes that were peeping from her shoes with solemn contemplation. Winter was here, and most of it to come, as Granny had said that morning. When these shoes were worn out, she would have to stop school. And she couldn't help them wearing. She did her best to pick the best trail going down the mountain every morning, but there were always hidden stones and treacherous roots to trip her. Try as she might, she could not prevent many an unlucky stumble that left its mark on the sturdy little shoes that trudged the trail in all kinds of weather.

If it were only summertime now, there would be blackberries in the hollow and huckleberries on the mountainside which she could pick for selling. She had bought her blue gingham dress this way, as well as her Reader and Spelling Book. Oh yes, if it were only summer, she could buy a new pair of shoes for herself. She could not hope for Granny to get another pair. The winters were long on the mountain, and there were many rocks. Granny needed new things,

When these shoes were worn out, she would have to stop school.

too. She couldn't go to Big Meeting because her gray coat had worn too thin. But Granny never said much about that. She went about her work as cheerfully as if she were always expecting a piece of good luck to come her way.

Mary Ellen could not be so cheerful. To think of having to give up school with all the long winter before her, and her class just halfway through long division—a big tear dropped in the sunlight before she knew it was on the way.

Granny came with an empty bucket. "You'll have to fetch water, honey," she said. "There's not enough in the house to soak the shucky beans." Shucky beans are green beans dried in the "shuck" or hull. Mary Ellen took the cedar bucket and hurried down the trail to the spring. Although the air was crisp, almost chill, the morning sun streaming down the mountain was warm and pleasant on her as she swung down the steep, rocky trail. So bent was she upon picking her way, avoiding the sharp stones which ruined shoes quickly, that she did not see the man sitting in front of the springhouse till he spoke to her.

"Good morning!" he said, nodding, and waved a friendly hand, which Mary Ellen noticed held a pencil. On his lap he had a large piece of paper. What in the world, she thought, was he trying to do? She was so surprised she forgot to speak, but the man was speaking again.

"I hope you'll excuse me camping here in your way—I've absolutely blocked your path, I see. But I must have this delightful little log house, and this is the best view of it."

Mary Ellen, coming closer, saw the sketch he held on his knee.

"Oh," she cried involuntarily. "How could anyone make, with just a few lines, so good a picture?"

"You like it then?" the man asked, sensing the wonder and admiration in her voice.

"You must be an artist—I've read of them!" she said, all her old shyness gone in her surprise at what she saw.

"Well, perhaps I am," he replied, "but there are those who doubt my ability—Mrs. Poget, for one. She declared that my pictures for her latest book leave much to be desired. That's why her publishers have shipped me down here to acquire some local color— and a few frostbites and frozen whiskers while I am doing my duty."

He spoke in so droll yet mournful a tone that Mary Ellen could not help laughing.

"You had better come up to Granny's house and get warm," she said with true mountain hospitality.

At the cabin, Granny cut short her ballad when she saw them coming.

"Howdy!" she said with a shy kindliness shown to all outlander visitors. "Come in and set yourself by the fire."

The artist thanked her and took the chair she placed in the corner for him. He seemed to be home all at once, and in a few minutes, he was showing them the sketches he had made that morning.

"And they're going into a book, Granny!" Mary Ellen told the old woman, who kept shaking her head and saying, "Iffen that is not a sight to behold, there never could be one!"

While they were looking at the pictures, the artist looked at Granny, at Mary Ellen, and all about the clean little cabin. He started to speak, then seemed to lose his words. "I wish— I'd like—" he said, and faltered as if he hardly knew how to go on with what he was saying.

Granny Allen came to his aid. "Might you want a drink of water, Stranger?" She reached for the gourd dipper hanging on a nail, but the artist man waved a denial of thirst.

"Will you pose for me?" he blurted out.

Both Mary Ellen and Granny looked helplessly at him and then at each other. "Let me make your pictures," said the artist, sensing their mystification. "I need you for this new book. I want this lovely pine cabin, and that stone fireplace, and the kettle on the crane. Of course, I will pay you for the privilege. And I'll try not to be in the way. Just let me have the chimney corner for a few days."

They consented at once for the "picture taking," as Granny Allen called it, though she declared it was "highway robbery" to take the man's money for less than nothing, but at last she gave in.

Those were interesting days which followed for Granny and Mary Ellen. When school was out, the little girl would hurry up the trail homeward, for she knew the artist man would be sitting in his corner making a picture of Granny, or perhaps a corner of the cabin itself, or the fire with the kettle on it.

It was fun to peep over his shoulder as he worked. The picture seemed to come effortlessly on the paper before him. Here a line, there a line—and then it was before you.

It was not hard to sit still for him when he was making pictures of her, because while he worked away with his pencil, he told such wonderful stories. He always had to read the stories for which he made pictures before they went into books and magazines— and he had read a great many.

When the pictures were done, the artist thanked Mary Ellen and Granny.

"You are nicer than any story people I know," he said when he was leaving.

Then he gave them a handful of silver apiece. They had never seen so much money at one time in all their lives.

"Buy something you want with this," he told them.

"A new coat to wear on Big Meeting days," said Granny, looking at her money.

"A pair of new shoes for me," said Mary Ellen, "so I can go to school all winter!"

6

When Mary Ellen Went to Town

One Saturday morning, bright and early, Uncle
Tobe's one-horse wagon rumbled down the mountain
and stopped at Granny Allen's door. Mary Ellen was
washing her face—they had not eaten breakfast yet—
and she gave three hasty flips with the towel and ran
to open the door, for she knew it was Uncle Tobe who
was there. She knew the sound of his wagon.

He came in slapping his hands together, for the
frosty air had nipped his fingers even through the red
yarn gloves he had on.

"Come up to our fire," Granny said. "We have not
had breakfast. You are just in time to have a cup of
good, hot coffee."

"Oh, I've eaten—long ago," the old man said, but
his nose sniffed the fragrance from the steaming
coffee pot that sat on a little bed of embers on one
side of the wide hearth opposite the old-fashioned
oven. At this moment, Granny took a pair of hooks
and lifted the oven lid carefully, disclosing the brown
biscuits within.

"Come and set your feet under the table," she

commanded Uncle Tobe. "Mary Ellen and I want our breakfast, and you might as well eat a bite with us for company."

"Oh, please do!" Mary Ellen begged him.

"Well—" Uncle Tobe hesitated, "I will, to please you all, but I'm not the least mite hungry!"

Granny poured him a cup of coffee, strong and black as he liked it. Mary Ellen passed him butter and honey to eat with the hot brown biscuits. As Uncle Tobe ate, he told them why he had stopped at their house that morning. He was going to Crossville with a load of kindling wood and could get anything that they needed.

"Prices are cheaper in town," he said, "than they are at the store on Near-Side. The storekeeper there has to charge more on account of the haul up the mountain."

Granny considered. "Mary Ellen needs shoes. And I have saved three dollars—that's what they cost at the store here. Maybe it would be a saving if I let you get them in Crossville for her."

"I'll be glad to do that," Uncle Tobe told her. He was eating with a "coming" appetite, he declared, buttering his third biscuit. Mary Ellen passed the honey jar to him. Granny poured another cup of coffee.

"Won't it be a mite of trouble, now?" she asked him. "You are all the time doing us a favor. I don't want to ride a free horse to death."

"Oh, it won't be a *smidgen* of trouble," Uncle Tobe

declared. "Just you give me Mary Ellen's shoe number, and I'll bring back the new shoes around four o'clock."

And now arose a great problem. Granny didn't know the number of Mary Ellen's shoes—neither did Mary Ellen! The shoes she had on were the ones she had worn from home on the other side of the mountain when she came to live with Granny and go to school here.

Uncle Tobe squinted an eye and regarded Mary Ellen's old shoes thoughtfully.

"Maybe I could guess at them," he said, but he said it very doubtfully. Then he had a better idea. "I tell you what," he said brightly, "Mary Ellen can come along with me. There's plenty of room for her right on the front seat up by me. Then she's sure to get shoes to fit her."

"Oh—oh—Granny! May I go?" Mary Ellen was delighted at the idea of going to town. She had never been to Crossville, but she had heard of it a long time. It was a very large village, almost a town, with several stores, rows of painted houses, and a train that went through the place twice a day. Mary Ellen had never seen a painted house until she went to school at the Mission. And she hadn't ever seen a train in her life. Oh, wouldn't it be exciting to go with Uncle Tobe! And Granny, seeing how eager she was about it, consented to let her make the trip, and set about to help her get ready.

"Thank you, Granny—oh, you are so good!"

"Put on your blue yarn dress," she said, "and the new red cap and mittens." These last articles Granny had made for her to wear on Sunday and special meeting days—but this was a special occasion.

While Mary Ellen dressed by the fire, Uncle Tobe went out to his wagon, and Granny packed Mary Ellen a lunch in her school basket. It was a very pretty basket made of wild honeysuckle vines, with a strong handle to carry it by and a tightly fitting cover.

When Mary Ellen was ready to start, Granny gave her the money—three dollars to buy her shoes.

"You may get them a little cheaper," she said, "but you better take this much along. If there happens to be a little left over, you may have it to spend for something you like—but don't waste your money."

"Thank you, Granny—oh, you are so good!" Mary Ellen hugged her, bade her goodbye, and ran to get into the wagon.

"Get up, Bijah!" Uncle Tobe shook the lines, and the wagon started on down the mountain with a great deal of noise. Bumpety-bump!

"Sit as tight as you can," Uncle Tobe advised her. "Better hold to the wagon seat with one hand and hang onto me with the other till we get over the steepest part."

Mary Ellen didn't mind the rough way, however. She scarcely noticed the bumping. All that she really felt was joy over their wonderful adventure. The sun rose over the highest peak of Big Log Mountain and turned the wooded slopes of it into red and golden patterns of beauty. The sun brought warmth and comfort, too. Mary Ellen hunched over to let its rays warm her back and stop the chills running between her shoulders.

She knew when they were approaching the village. They had entered a road less rocky and rough than that over which they had come. The hollow lane widened to a valley. The houses were not log cabins here, but were what Uncle Tobe called "frame" buildings. Only a few women that they had passed on the road were wearing sunbonnets—instead, they were wearing hats and looked dressed up as if it were Sunday.

How thrilling it was to drive between the rows of painted houses which looked so funny and crowded together, with hardly any room at all between them.

Uncle Tobe stopped in front of some of these houses, and Mary Ellen stayed with the wagon while he went in to see if they needed kindling wood. Sometimes they did, and sometimes they didn't. But on the whole, Uncle Tobe had good luck. By dinnertime, the wagon was empty.

"Now we'll see about your shoes," Uncle Tobe said. They went into a store, and the clerk tried to fit Mary Ellen. But the only pair he had that would do was too high—five dollars!

"Come on," said Uncle Tobe. "Let's go to the store where I buy brogans and overalls. It's a good place, and the prices are right."

Here were shoes—dozens of pairs, all arranged on tables and counters. Shoes of all kinds, from workman's brogans to little shoes for wee babies.

"We're having a special shoe sale today," a heavy, good-natured man told them. "Look around and pick out a pair. You'll never buy any shoes cheaper. Half-price and less."

Mary Ellen had no trouble finding a pair to fit her. And such pretty shoes, so black and shiny. She looked at them with longing, afraid to ask the price of them, afraid they would cost more money than the three dollar bills she had wadded tight down in the corner of her pocket.

Perhaps Uncle Tobe guessed her thoughts. "How much?" He asked the question for her.

The salesman glanced at a tag on the shoes. "These are a special bargain. An odd pair. Just a dollar and a half—formerly sold for three dollars."

Mary Ellen drew a deep breath and hugged the shoes to her. So she could buy them after all! She had more than enough money. Why, she had a whole dollar and a half left! And that would be all her money. She could spend it as she pleased—Granny had said so. Oh, that was a lot of money.

What could she get with it? A new dress? A stylish

hat to wear on Sunday? These would be nice. Then
she had another thought. She would buy a surprise for
Granny. Granny Allen had made her the new cap and
the mittens to match. Granny had saved the money
for her shoes. It had taken a long time to do it—a
nickel, a dime every now and then in the blue teapot
in the cupboard. Granny needed new shoes herself—
she would buy a pair of new shoes for Granny if she
possibly could. She consulted Uncle Tobe. Did he
think she would have enough money? Uncle Tobe
consulted the clerk. The clerk went around the shoe
counter, picking up shoes of various kinds.

"What size do you want?" he asked them. Mary
Ellen looked dismayed. She hadn't the least idea what
number Granny wore. Here, indeed, was a problem
worse than the one which had come up at the
breakfast table that morning. And what in the world
could they do about it?

Uncle Tobe had a bright idea—just as he'd had
that morning.

"She wears a number six," he declared, "the very
same size as my Hannah. I know because they've
borrowed each other's shoes at times to wear to
Big Meeting."

The clerk hunted for a number six which he could
sell Mary Ellen for as little as a dollar and a half. For
a time he looked discouraged, and Mary Ellen looked
discouraged, too. Then, suddenly he brightened.

"Here they are!" he shouted. "The very thing. Nice pair of shoes for a lady. Salvaged in a big fire—but not the least bit damaged. Price one dollar and a half— and a great big bargain!"

Mary Ellen paid him the rest of her money. There wouldn't be any extra pennies to buy something else for herself, but what did that matter? She had the lovely new shoes to wear home, she had the ride in Uncle Tobe's wagon, and she had something to take home to Granny. She needed nothing more to make her happy.

7

Mary Ellen's Party Dress

"Granny," asked Mary Ellen one day as soon as she came home from school, "did you ever go to a party—a dress-up party?"

Granny Allen looked up from the quilt squares which she was piecing together and regarded Mary Ellen with a twinkle in her eye.

"Yes, indeed! I used to go to parties," she replied while her fingers stroked the bright print pieces in her lap. "Why, this very piece of sprigged challis was a piece I bought to wear to a party once. A long-wearing pattern it was, too. I wore it to every wedding and picnic and Big Meeting I went to on Big Log Mountain for at least ten years—or longer."

"They are going to have a party at school," Mary Ellen told Granny. "They are going to dress up like folks in books. It's to celebrate Book Week," she added. "Book Week, you know, Granny," she went on, "is a special week in November when we read new books and learn about the authors who wrote them."

Granny Allen listened attentively, for although she had little book knowledge, she had great respect for

it and was always ready to listen to Mary Ellen's talk
about school and the things she was learning.

"I read *Heidi* this week, Granny," Mary Ellen told
her. "It's about a little mountain girl like me. Her
home was in the Swiss Alps, and, see, I brought it
home to read to you if you like." As she spoke, she
held up the storybook so that Granny could see the
picture of Heidi on the bright paper cover.

"Looks a lot like you," Granny Allen remarked,
"with her wild hair flying and her bright red cheeks
shining like Winesap apples."

"Oh, Granny, do you think so?" Mary Ellen almost
shouted. "Then I'll be Heidi at the Book Week party.
Miss Ellison told us that we might dress up like any
book person we fancied. I'd rather be Heidi than any
other storybook person that I have ever heard or
read about."

"If you had a dress like that," said Granny, "you'd
look as alike as two peas in a pod. That's the truth, and
no mistaking."

Mary Ellen regarded Heidi's pretty dress and
glanced at her own faded gingham.

"I wish I had a dress like hers," she said.

Granny heard a wistful note, and she tried to think
of something comforting, but she couldn't think of
anything but, "Yes, dearie, I wish it, too."

Mary Ellen went to pick up chips and gather up
a basket full. Granny said the oak chips made the

very best coals to bake corn pone on the fire. This
afternoon Mary Ellen was hungry. When she went
back into the house, she looked in the cupboard for
some bread. Not a piece she could find. And how
hungry she was! Granny heard her prowling around
and guessed at once what she was after.

"I gave the last scrap to the chickens," she
explained. "But my own chick must be fed. Come, cut
some quilt pieces for me a while, and I'll make some
fresh cornbread."

Mary Ellen took Granny's rocking chair and began
to cut as she was told, being very careful to follow the
pattern and to keep her edges smooth.

Meanwhile, Granny brought the little Dutch oven
and set it on the hearth, with a shovelful of coals
underneath to heat it. The lid she placed on the fire.
Mary Ellen sniffed as the oven was greased round
and round again with a piece of bacon rind to keep
the bread from sticking. My, but that smell was good!
Plop—plop—she heard the corn dodgers being patted
into place. Cling! went the oven lid on top. Cling!
went the iron hooks as they rattled on their nail again.
Rattle—rattle! went a shovelful of coals.

"There!" said Granny. "It's on. Now I must go and
milk the cow. It's getting to be chore time. You might
cut a few more quilt pieces while you sit there and
watch the bread."

"All the pretty dress pieces are used up, Granny,"
Mary Ellen said.

"Those are the leftovers," Granny told her. "I found the old dress the other day, down in the bottom of the cedar chest, where I had put it away many, many years ago. It's as bright and pretty as the day I wore it to Lavina Lowry's quilting party. But I couldn't get into it today—I've grown all around if I haven't grown up." Granny Allen was not tall—not much taller than Mary Ellen—but she certainly was bigger all around! Now she brought the yellow sprigged challis from a peg behind the cupboard door.

"Might as well use it in the quilt," she said. "It'll look real pretty on a bed."

Then she took her milk bucket and hurried outside, for the cow was calling from the shed.

Mary Ellen threw a pine knot on the fire and stood up in its light to hold the dress at arm's length. Oh, it was a pretty dress! Quaint tight waist, full-gathered skirt, and strange little puffed-out sleeves. It looked something like ones she had seen in storybooks. It looked a lot like Heidi's dress! At this thought, Mary Ellen danced up and down.

"I believe it would do!" she said in a whisper to herself. In a moment, the dress was over her head. Yes, it fitted, almost perfectly. A little too long, but they could fix that. With a kerchief or scrap around her neck, she would make a very good Heidi, indeed. And wouldn't everyone be surprised!

She looked like something from a storybook.

Granny Allen was surprised that minute as she stepped through the door.

"Gracious goodness!" she cried, almost dropping her pail. "How you nearly scared me, child! For a minute, I thought I was seeing myself from long ago!"

But she liked Mary Ellen in her old party dress. "Of course, you may wear it," she said. "I'm downright pleased that you can use it. But hurry, Honey, look at that bread!"

Yes, it was burned a little on one side but not enough to matter much, not to Mary Ellen, anyway. She was happy enough to eat burned crusts as if they were perfectly golden.

And now Mary Ellen could hardly wait for the Book Week party. She told no one but Lovie Lane about her Heidi dress. Lovie had a secret of her own which she shared with Mary Ellen. She was coming to the party as Little Red Riding Hood. She hadn't a new dress, but her mother was going to dye her old coat and knit a cap to match it.

"Oh," Mary Ellen told her, "you'll look lovely, a sure-enough fancy-fine Red Riding Hood!"

"I can hardly wait," said Lovie, "to see you dressed like Heidi!" They called each other by these storybook names all through Book Week, just for fun.

Meanwhile, the whole school was busy as a beehive getting ready for the party. The teacher brought fun posters to put in the schoolroom. From papers and magazines, the children made many of their own. They painted their reading table and made new jackets for the old books, so they all looked nice and clean.

There were not many flowers in the woods they could get for decorating, just a few frostbitten wild asters and sprays of goldenrod. But the walls were hung with pine boughs and sprays of spruce and cedar, and the floor was scrubbed with water and sand till it shone like a looking glass.

"The schoolhouse looks as if it *knew* there was going to be a party in it," Mary Ellen said, and everybody laughed.

At last, the great day came. Friends and fathers and mothers came to hear the program which the children had prepared. This was made up mostly of songs and storytelling. A few of the little ones said pieces out of *Mother Goose*. Each had done their best to dress for their part in a suitable manner. Little Boy Blue wore blue overalls and a shirt to match and carried his daddy's hunting horn, which he blew in a mighty manner at the right place. The six-year-old Thomas twins, Billy and Betty, were Jack and Jill and carried a big water bucket, which dropped at the wrong time and rolled clear off the stage!

The older children told stories about their favorite book people. There was one about Robinson Crusoe,

another of Huckleberry Finn. Several girls chose
character parts out of *Little Women* and gave a scene
from the book which they had made into a play.

Lovie Lane leaned over and whispered to Mary
Ellen: "I'm scared! I know I'll forget my piece—and it
comes next!"

"Don't be afraid. I'll help you out if you forget," said
Mary Ellen. "Just remember that you are Red Riding
Hood, and then maybe you won't forget!"

But she did. Lovie always forgot her school pieces
after she got up, no matter how well she knew them
before! So Mary Ellen helped her out, two or three
times, as usual.

And now it was *her* turn.

"Here comes Heidi!" she thought as she went up
front in the pretty party dress Granny had given her.

As she started to tell her story, she saw Granny
smiling from her seat in the very front row. Mary
Ellen smiled back.

"I must do my best—for Granny," she thought.

And her best must have been very good, indeed.
Everyone said so.

8

Mary Ellen's Thanksgiving Dinner

The weather was growing colder and colder on Big Log Mountain. "The leaves turned early this fall," said Granny Allen. "Winter is on his way."

Granny Allen always spoke of winter as if he were a traveler coming from far away to visit around their fireside. Not so welcome, to be sure, as the other seasons, but a visitor whose coming was to be expected and whose long stay required preparation.

But there had been little preparations this year. Ill fortune had befallen them. First, Daisy, the yellow cow, had gone dry a month ago. The reason, as Granny said, was because she had eaten white acorns, which do not agree with cows at all, though they are fine food for pigs. Then a stray mule had broken through the fence and eaten up their late roasting ears one day when they were away from home. The vegetables in their little garden were gone by the last of September. Only the sweet potato patch remained, but they were thankful indeed to have plenty of potatoes for food. Sweet potatoes would keep in their underground dugout all winter long, and here they stored them away on a Saturday when Mary Ellen could be at home to help.

Granny was right about winter coming so early. It came ahead of time this year, with the first snow early in November and a bigger one for Thanksgiving Day.

It began to snow three days before Thanksgiving, and Mary Ellen had to stay at home the first stormy day. The snow fell so fast, it was like a thick curtain. She could not have found the trail down the mountain. It snowed all day and all night. On the morning of the second day, no sign of any trail was to be seen.

"Oh, I'll have to stay home another day!" sighed Mary Ellen. "And I'll get behind in my headmarks."

But better luck came that day. Uncle Tobe Carr came along with his sled on his way to the mill. He stopped to ask Granny Allen if she needed to have a turn of corn ground, and Mary Ellen got a ride to school.

When she went in that morning a bit late, Miss Ellison was telling the children about Thanksgiving.

Thanksgiving! Mary Ellen gave a start. "Is *this* Thanksgiving Day?" she whispered to Lovie Lane.

"No, but tomorrow is," Lovie replied.

There was to be no school tomorrow so that all the folks on the mountain could eat Thanksgiving dinner at home or visit their neighbors and kin.

Mary Ellen remembered that last year Granny said she had cooked a fine dinner of chicken and dumplings and pumpkin pie. And some neighbors had come to eat with her—Uncle Tobe Carr and his wife, Aunt Hannah. Mary Ellen was very much afraid that she and Granny wouldn't have a regular Thanksgiving dinner this year. The chickens had mostly been sold to buy winter clothes for the two of them, and as for pumpkin pie—the stray mule had gobbled up their one big pumpkin to finish off his meal of roasting ears.

Uncle Tobe stopped to get her that afternoon on his way back up the mountain, and as they rode up the trail, they talked about Thanksgiving Day. Uncle Tobe remembered his dinner last year—the pumpkin pie especially.

"I had *three pieces!*" he said with a chuckle. "If your Granny makes a pumpkin pie this year, save me a piece, will you?"

Then Mary Ellen had to tell him, of course, about the mule getting the pumpkin.

"So there won't be any pumpkin pie for Thanksgiving dinner this year."

"Too bad, too bad." Uncle Tobe was very sympathetic. "The stray mule didn't bother me— but a bunch of stray pigs did, and ruined my sweet potatoes."

"Too bad," Mary Ellen sighed, sympathizing with Uncle Tobe in her turn. Then they were both quiet for a while. All at once, Mary Ellen had a plan—the merest idea of a plan it was, but it was a plan, anyway. She couldn't keep it; it seemed too good.

"Uncle Tobe!" She spoke so suddenly that the old man nearly dropped his lines, and the red ox pulling the sled stopped in his tracks in the middle of the road.

"What—what is the matter?" stammered Uncle Tobe.

"I've got a new plan," was the reply. "I was thinking about Thanksgiving dinner and wondering if Granny would invite you and Aunt Hannah—when we didn't have any pumpkin pie—or anything much but sweet potatoes. And then I thought we could swap some sweet potatoes for a pumpkin, maybe. Do you like potatoes?" she asked a bit anxiously.

"I do that!" exclaimed the old man. "It's a fine plan if it suits your granny."

The plan pleased Granny Allen well.

"That's the way we used to do in the old days," she said. "And I call it a neighborly fashion."

Mary Ellen was happy indeed to think that her Thanksgiving plan was working out so well. At first, she feared that Granny might not like it. But it seemed that she did.

"I'll be down in the morning," said Uncle Tobe, starting on his way, "and get some potatoes for my dinner, and give you a pumpkin in exchange."

So far, Mary Ellen's plan had turned out well— but it turned out even better, as you shall see. The next morning, while Granny Allen and Mary Ellen were eating breakfast by the fire, they heard a shout outside.

"Hello! Hello!"

"It's Uncle Tobe," cried Mary Ellen, running to unlatch the door.

"It's Aunt Hannah, too!" she cried as soon as she got the door open. Yes, there were both of their old neighbors, smiling in the doorway.

"A surprise party!" said Aunt Hannah. She had a big bundle in her arms. "I thought that since we were swapping pumpkin and potatoes, we might as well swap our dinners—and cook and eat them together!" she explained. She had brought a fat chicken along, and several other things as well.

Wasn't Granny Allen surprised and pleased!

And that is how Mary Ellen's plans turned into a whole Thanksgiving dinner. She had two pieces of pie—and Uncle Tobe had three. They both liked pumpkin pie.

9

Potluck

Mary Ellen came in from the pine patch, where she had gone to pick up kindling, and found Granny sorting out herbs on the kitchen table.

"Shut the door quick, honey, or the wind will blow these dry leaves together, and I won't know Solomon's Seal from wintergreen. And that would be awful, for I might give somebody the wrong kind of medicine sometime."

Mary Ellen shut the door in a hurry and came over to the table.

"Is somebody sick, Granny?"

The old woman separated a few bits of snakeroot from some dried sprigs of pennyroyal before she answered Mary Ellen.

"Yes, Aunt Viney Grigsby was taken down real bad a while ago and has sent for me to come and see her. Uncle John brought word on his way to the mill. I've got to set off in a hurry, and I'll be back just as quick as I can. There's not a thing for your dinner, but you can roast some potatoes in the fire. You know how to do that, and there's plenty of milk in the big brown jar, and butter in the corner cupboard. You'll get along till I get back. It's past the middle of the morning by the sun crack on the floor. It's no more than five miles to Aunt Viney's. I'll be back by sundown, anyway, and in time to make bread for supper."

As the old woman spoke, she went busily about the cabin making hurried preparations for the trip to the other side of Big Log Mountain to visit her sick neighbor. It was late in autumn and a chilly day, so she wrapped about her shoulders a shawl which had turned the wind and rain for fifty years and over. On her head, she tied an old gray hood instead of the black sateen bonnet, which was saved for go-to-meeting wear and other special occasions.

"Now that I'm ready, I reckon I'll mosey along. Get along the best you can, Honey. There's plenty of wood to keep a good fire. Play and piddle about all you want to, and if you get lonesome, you can pass the time away piecing on 'Jacob's Ladder.'"

This was a quilt which Mary Ellen was making under Granny's direction and designed to go into the cedar chest, which was Granny's most prized possession, containing quilts old and new and all well made, and beautiful. Nothing pleased Mary Ellen more than to look at the cheerful array of quilts on the days when she helped Granny to air them. Mary Ellen herself had pieced one, a nine-patch pattern called "The Churn Dasher." That had been quite easy.

"Jacob's Ladder" was a prettier pattern, and a bit more difficult, too.

After Granny had gone, Mary Ellen got the broom from the corner and swept the floor where Granny had scattered little bits of her herbs. Then she piled a few chunks on the fire between the backlog and forestick. The sun was shining, the day was clear, but the air was crisp this morning, and the open door that let in the light let in a lot of cold air with it.

Mary Ellen stood on the hearth and warmed first one side and then another while she considered the next thing to do. It wasn't quite time to get dinner. The potatoes would roast in less than an hour. The sun path lengthened slowly across the planks of the kitchen floor from one crack to another. Granny Allen had no clock, but she had taught Mary Ellen to read the sun cracks on the floor. When the sun reached the crack in the middle of the floor, it was counted high noon and time to eat dinner. Plenty of time yet to play or to piece on the "Jacob's Ladder" quilt. Which should it be first? Mary Ellen was still undecided when someone looked in at the door and said, "Good morning!"

"Oh, Miss Ellison!" Mary Ellen thought that it was her teacher from the Mission until she looked straight into her visitor's face.

"No, not Miss Ellison this time. I'm Miss Ferry, the new teacher, and I'm out visiting folks this morning, trying to get acquainted."

"Is—oh, is Miss Ellison gone?" Mary Ellen faltered, and in her distress at the thought of this came near to forgetting her manners. She did recover herself enough to say, "Come in," and the lady hopped up on the stone which served for a step and came on up to the fire.

"Oh, how good this feels!" she exclaimed. Then she looked at Mary Ellen, whose face suggested a question mark.

"Oh, excuse me! You asked me a question. No, Miss Ellison is not gone. I'm an extra teacher at the Mission. We're going to have a class in sewing and one in cooking, too, for a while."

Mary Ellen thought this would be fine.

"Do we eat the things we cook?" she asked her visitor.

"Oh, yes," was the laughing reply. "We shall gobble it up immediately—if it is good enough to eat."

Miss Ferry said she came from Pittsburgh.

"I know where that is," said Mary Ellen. "It's a big city in Pennsylvania. It's on the map in my Geography. We had it in our lesson just last week."

Then she saw that the sun had crept across the floor till it touched the crack in the middle. That meant it was dinnertime, and she hadn't a thing for dinner! She hadn't even put the potatoes to roast. Mary Ellen was perplexed. She knew that it was good manners to ask her visitor to stay for dinner—but since there wasn't anything to eat, she wondered what she really ought to do. After a minute, she decided.

"Granny's gone for the day," she said. "She didn't have time to get dinner, and I don't know how to cook very well—but I'm going to roast some potatoes. Do you like potatoes roasted in ashes?"

"I do!" Miss Ferry assured Mary Ellen. "And if that is an invitation, I'll certainly stay and have dinner with you. I'm really very hungry."

Mary Ellen got some Irish potatoes and buried them in the hot ashes between the big andirons to bake. By and by they would be ready to eat. But Mary Ellen was wishing that there was something else she could cook since she had company for dinner.

Miss Ferry was looking at the kitchen walls hung with strings of dried beans and onions, pumpkin rings, and pepper pods.

"I have just been thinking of something," she said to Mary Ellen suddenly. "I'd like to earn my dinner by cooking something nice for you."

Mary Ellen's eyes opened wide and wider when she heard this. It sounded very nice, she was thinking, but Miss Ferry was her company. She shouldn't have to cook her own dinner!

"All these good things before my eyes! I can't wait any longer, Mary Ellen. Get me a pot, and let me get to work!"

After that, things happened in a hurry. Mary Ellen found the little black pot which set in the chimney corner when it wasn't swinging on the crane. Miss Ferry had a skilled hand. She popped into the kettle a little bit of this and that: beans, onions, potatoes—and no telling what else! At last, the pot was set swinging on the crane above the leaping flames.

"When that's done, we'll have dinner," Miss Ferry said to Mary Ellen.

"What do you call it?" Mary Ellen asked. "It isn't soup—or is it?"

Miss Ferry laughed. "No, it's not exactly soup. In fact, it's something quite different from anything I've ever made before. Let's wait until we eat it, and then perhaps we can think of a name."

Mary Ellen thought this very funny—to eat something without a name. But still, it was very interesting to think about it, and watch it cook, and sniff the good smell from the kettle that bubbled as if it were in a hurry to get done as soon as it could for their dinner.

While they waited, Mary Ellen entertained her guest by showing her the quilt-piecing—her nine-patch "Churn Dasher," and the one called "Jacob's Ladder." Miss Ferry thought both of them very pretty.

"You do neat work, Mary Ellen. Soon you will be making dresses to wear!"

Mary Ellen entertained her guest by showing her the
quilt-piecing.

Mary Ellen blushed at these praises and thought she would have to tell this to Granny when she came. But now she must give her attention to those potatoes which ought to be done.

She raked away the coals and embers and found them to be well done—only one was burned a little. The smells from the pot tempted a taste.

"Nearly done it is!" said Miss Ferry as she lifted the lid and took a bite. "Let's get the table set, Mary Ellen."

Mary Ellen got out the clean white cloth made out of homespun linen and called by Granny "the company spread." She knew that Granny would be willing. This teacher was certainly company—and besides, she had helped get the dinner!

Just as they were sitting down, who should come in but Granny! And what a surprise it was to her! What a surprise to see the dinner and Mary Ellen having company! And, as for Mary Ellen and the new teacher, they were also surprised to have Granny Allen back in time for dinner, but everybody was happy to sit down. They were all hungry, and they ate and talked at the same time, and made many explanations.

Aunt Viney was much better, and Granny had come back early. She said she did wish she had come back sooner to get a better dinner.

"Oh, but this *is* a better dinner, Granny!" Mary Ellen was eating something that tasted very good indeed. "It is a much better dinner than I was going to

Everybody was happy to sit down.

have by myself. The new teacher cooked it, Granny, in the little black pot. What about that!"

Granny thought it a wonder that the new teacher could cook anything that they had in the house to taste like this food on their plates.

"What do you call it?" asked Granny. "It's some kind of stew, isn't it?"

"We haven't named it yet," the visitor said. "Mary Ellen and I were so busy getting things ready to go into the pot that we decided to name it later."

"I'd like to know how you made it—whatever you call it," said Granny. "You'll have to teach Mary Ellen at school, and she can tell me all about it."

When Miss Ferry started to go, Granny gave her an invitation: "Come back and potluck with us again," she said.

"I have thought of something!" cried Mary Ellen, jumping up and clapping her hands. "Let's call what we cooked in the kettle *Potluck*—for it was so lucky to have it to go with the potatoes!"

10

Christmas Music

Down at the Mission school, they were getting ready for Christmas. The children were learning Christmas carols and Christmas recitations.

Mary Ellen was learning "The Night Before Christmas." And Lovie Lane was trying to learn "Away in a Manger."

"That's not a regular piece to say—it's a song," said Mary Ellen.

"I'm going to *say* it," Lovie replied, "because I think it's pretty, and it won't take long to learn."

Lovie never said long recitations, while Mary Ellen liked that kind. She scorned anything short and easy. How she loved the Christmas songs, and to stand by the little old organ and sing to the marvelous music it made! She led the other children. It was easy for her to carry a tune. She had a good ear for music, and the words of the songs made pictures in her mind so that she could not forget them.

One day Miss Ellison told the school that some outlander people were coming to visit the Mission on Christmas Eve, and Santa Claus was coming with them.

The little ones gave whoops of delight, and the older ones cheered for them, for everybody was thrilled to think of having company for Christmas.

Uncle Tobe Carr, who was chopping wood a little way down the mountain, rushed up to see if the house was on fire.

"What's all this hip-and-hurrah?" he cried as he burst through the door.

When he found that nothing was the matter, he sat down to hear the children sing awhile.

"Did you like the songs, Uncle Tobe?" Mary Ellen asked the old man as he walked along with her up the trail when school was over.

"I did for a fact," he replied. "I was thinking that very minute what pretty fiddle tunes they would make if I could rightly learn them."

"They are easy to learn," Mary Ellen said, and then to prove it to him, she sang to him her favorite song, "O Come, All Ye Faithful."

"That's a grand tune," said Uncle Tobe. "I could pick it up now and carry it along if I had my old fiddle."

At the parting of the ways, Uncle Tobe said, "Maybe we'll drop in after supper, and you can help me get that tune while my wife and your granny gossip."

"Come," Mary Ellen invited him, "we'll be right

glad to have you. Granny said this morning that she hadn't seen you for more than a month of Sundays."

That night Mary Ellen taught Uncle Tobe the tune, and he practiced it on his fiddle till he had it well enough to suit him. Then he wanted to learn another, but it had to wait until another time.

"It's getting late," said Aunt Hannah, lighting a pine torch to guide them home.

"You must come again soon," said Granny. "Come down as often as you can. I like to see my neighbors."

After that, Uncle Tobe and Aunt Hannah came in quite often after supper and sat with them until bedtime. Of course, he brought his fiddle, for as he told Mary Ellen, he had his mind set on learning some new tunes while he had a chance to do it.

Down at the Mission, preparations went on for the coming Christmas program. Day by day, time slipped by. The little ones counted on their fingers. At last they could count on one hand the days to come before Christmas. Christmas Eve and the Christmas tree! Christmas Eve and the program. Santa Claus and the outlander company. No wonder that lessons were half forgotten and then left off entirely for Christmas doings and holiday fun.

And then the bad luck happened—on the very last day of school it was, early in the morning, right in the middle of a Christmas song:

"O come, all ye faithful, joyful and triumphant—"

That night Mary Ellen taught Uncle Tobe the tune.

The organ stopped. The children stopped. They didn't know what was the matter. They asked the teacher, but she didn't know. The organ had simply stopped playing.

"Something has gone wrong inside of it," she said. "Something must have broken. It's a very, very old organ, you know."

But whatever was the matter couldn't very well be helped just then. They would have to get along without music.

Miss Ellison started the next song, and the children tried to follow, but somehow they didn't do very well. They were used to the music of the organ. Some of their voices sounded flat, some rather squeaky. None of them sounded very good.

Mary Ellen had an idea.

"Uncle Tobe can play for us!" she cried. "He has learned all the tunes on his fiddle!"

"Oh, if he will!" the teacher said.

"Oh, if he will!" echoed the children.

"I know he will," Mary Ellen said. "I know he will if I ask him."

The teacher allowed her to go right away, and Lovie Lane went along with her to keep her company on the way. When they came back down the mountain, Uncle Tobe was walking between them, and he was bringing his fiddle.

"Thank you for coming!" Miss Ellison told him.

"Thank you!" chorused the children.

"You're all right welcome," Uncle Tobe replied, "but you'd better thank Mary Ellen, for she is the one who helped me to learn the Christmas tunes on my fiddle."

The Christmas program was a great success. The little schoolhouse was crowded with people who had come to see the Christmas tree and the Christmas exercises. Most of them had heard about Santa Claus, too, and the outlander folk who were expected, and they wanted to get a glimpse of them. Nobody felt disappointed. They saw all they had come to see and had several surprises.

The Christmas tree itself was a joy to behold, filling one corner of the room and hanging full of mysterious gifts which nobody but Santa knew anything about as yet. Yes, Santa Claus was present. He had come along with the outlander folk, and he did not act like a stranger. He shook hands with most of the grown people, and hugged and kissed the babies, and went about patting everybody on the head.

There was so much fun and excitement, it was a wonder the children could remember their Christmas songs and recitations when the time came, but they did—they did! In fact, they did much better than they had ever done before. It may have been Uncle Tobe's fiddle that started them right and kept them going. Yes, it may have been the fiddle—and it may have been Santa Claus who was their inspiration.

At any rate, everything went well. No one forgot his recitation or failed to carry out his part in a song. And each one was rewarded with some of the fruit on the Christmas tree.

"What did you get, Mary Ellen?" Lovie asked as they stood together after the program was over.

"I haven't opened anything yet," was the answer. "But I think that one is a dolly. This big bundle must be a storybook—and I smell some peppermint candy."

11

Hominy and Sassafras Tea

Mary Ellen swung the chip basket lightly and started for the woodpile. It certainly did take a lot of chips to cook a pot of hominy. A chip fire, declared Granny Allen, was the best kind for cooking hominy. A few chips—a low fire, and the kettle boiled away hour after hour until at last the hominy was done.

When Mary Ellen came back with the chips, Granny was tying on her bonnet, the black sateen one she wore on meeting days, and she had her Sunday coat on. Mary Ellen was so surprised that she dropped the basket and spilled chips all over the floor.

"Oh, oh!" she cried in dismay, but Granny didn't scold her.

"You can sweep them up a little later," she said. "But now you must help me get off. I'm going down to the Mission to see that Boston woman who is visiting Miss Ellison. They say she is buying old things and paying an outlandish price. I have a mind to sell the blue teapot. It ought to be old enough. Came from England. My great-grandmother brought it clear across the stormy waters, and they say she held it in

her lap the whole enduring way! You take it down
from the cupboard shelf and dust it real careful, while
I count these eggs Miss Ellison wants."

Mary Ellen did as she was told. When the
blue teapot was dusted, Granny wrapped it in a
piece of blanket cloth and packed it in the basket
with the eggs.

"I'll be back by dinner time," she said. "You keep
the chip fire going, and when I come back, we'll have
hominy for dinner and a cup of sassafras tea."

Mary Ellen clapped her hands. "Oh, goody, goody!"
It was a special treat to have sassafras tea—and in the
middle of the week, not a company day or Sunday!

"I'll keep up the fire, Granny," she promised.

"Just the way I showed you," Granny said. "A few
chips right under the pot so the sides won't scorch
and burn, and put in a little water now and then."

"Yes," said Mary Ellen, "I'll remember
that, Granny."

The first thing she did after Granny was gone was
to sweep the cabin floor. Then she mended the fire
and peeped into the pot. The water was bubbling low.
Empty bucket—she must run to the spring.

As she skipped down the trail to the spring, she
swung the bucket to the tune of the old ballad and
sang:

> "There lived an old lord
> by the Northern Sea,
> Bow-ee down!

There lived an old lord
by the Northern Sea,
Bow and balance to me!
There lived an old lord
by the Northern Sea,
And he had daughters,
one, two, three,
I'll be true to my love,
if my love'll be true to me!"

"Good morning!" Around the turn of the trail, she
almost ran into a lady whom she knew at once for
an outlander. She knew it by the way she said, "Good
morning," instead of "Howdy!" Also by the kind of
clothes she was wearing and by the walking stick she
was carrying. In the mountains, young women do not
need these.

"Good morning, my dear," said the lady. Anybody but an outlander would have said, "Howdy," or "Sissy." Yes, this was a woman from "far beyond," as Granny Allen called all the places beyond Big Log Mountain and the valley below. But Mary Ellen had manners.

"Good morning," she replied, and started on after her water, but the lady stood in the middle of the trail.

"I think I am lost," she said doubtfully. "I left the Mission to take a little walk. That was early in the morning, and when I turned back, I kept going and going—but I can't find the way—not the right one."

"The Mission's down there," said Mary Ellen, pointing in the right direction.

"I don't see it," the lady sighed.

"You can't for the trees," said Mary Ellen. "It's just beyond that spur of pines. It's not very far," she added. The poor young lady seemed tired and discouraged.

"Come up to our house and rest awhile," she said. "Granny will be back for dinner, and then I can go along and show you the way. I go to school there," she added.

"Oh, thank you," the young lady said gratefully. "I am leaving for Boston this afternoon. But I think they said the mail wagon would not be along before two o'clock. I must be at the Mission when it passes."

"That will be all right," said Mary Ellen. "I know a shortcut down the mountain."

She knew all at once who the young lady was.

"My Granny went to see you," she told her. "And she took the blue teapot that came from England across the stormy water."

"Oh, I am sorry!" exclaimed the young lady. "Do you think we could overtake her if we started back right now?"

"But we can't start out," said Mary Ellen. "I've got to get water for the hominy pot—and I've got to keep the chip fire going."

As it was, they got back barely in time to save the hominy from burning. The chip fire needed replenishing, too.

Mary Ellen tried to be polite. She gave her company Granny's rocker and showed her some of Granny's quilts, just as Granny did when the summer people came up to look at the things she made. Sometimes they bought a cover they liked, to take it back to the city, and that was very good luck indeed.

"What lovely quilts!" said the lady. "I do wish I had this morning-glory pattern. It would suit my blue bedroom perfectly."

"Granny made it to sell to a woman last year," Mary Ellen told her. "Then the woman changed her mind about it."

"Would she sell it to me?" The young lady laid loving hands on the cover, and her white fingers touched the morning glories as gently as fluttering butterflies. "Oh, *would* she let me have it?"

"For ten dollars," replied Mary Ellen. "See, here is the price pinned on it."

The young lady opened a beaded purse. "It's worth twice that much," she stated.

Mary Ellen looked at the money in her hands. Oh, wouldn't Granny be *happy*! And that minute, Granny came in at the door.

"I missed the—" Then she saw the lady sitting in her rocker beyond Mary Ellen, who proceeded to introduce them and to make the necessary explanations.

"You're the woman I'm after," said Granny. "Would you like to buy an old teapot?" And she carefully took off the wrapper from the bundle she held as carefully as if it had been a baby.

"It is beautiful," the lady said. "But to tell you the truth, I'd much rather have this beautiful coverlet I have just bought."

Granny Allen was indeed happy. "I've been wanting to sell that cover—and I *didn't* want to sell the blue teapot. I was going to let you have it to get money for Mary Ellen's school clothes. And now I don't need to do it."

Then, with true mountain courtesy, she invited the visitor to dinner. The hominy was quite done now, and Granny heaped a platter while Mary Ellen, from the blue teapot, poured the cups of sassafras tea.

12

The Last Day of School

The Mission school closed the middle of May when the Near-Side of Big Log Mountain was beautiful with the blossoming glory of laurel and wild azalea. The children gathered great armfuls of flowers to decorate the schoolhouse, for the last day was a great occasion, a neighborhood celebration.

The morning was spent in getting ready. The house was swept and dusted, windows washed, and everything put into most unusual order. The boys carried water from the spring, moved the heavy schoolroom furniture, and answered calls for help from the girls with unflagging zeal and good nature.

Mary Ellen and Lovie made laurel wreaths to hang above the windows, sitting in the pleasant shade of a pine so the flowers would not wither.

"I feel a little lonesome," Lovie said, "to think that school is over, and I won't get to see you every day. But I'll get to see you every Sunday, for Sunday school goes the whole year long."

Mary Ellen looked up at her friend.

"Listen, Lovie, I'll tell you something if you'll promise not to cry and spoil this last day we have together."

"Oh, Mary Ellen—you're not going home?" All at once, she guessed the secret, because it was the very thing she had been afraid would happen.

"Yes," said Mary Ellen. "Granny's going, too— going to Far-Side to stay all summer. Father's coming over this afternoon, and we're going back with him tomorrow."

"Oh, Mary Ellen!" Lovie cried. The thought of losing her playmate filled her heart with a passionate grief which overflowed in tears.

"Don't cry, Lovie. I'll tell you something else. I'm coming back with Granny to live with her and go to school again. And it won't be long till September."

Lovie thought three months and a half a long time, but it was a great consolation to know that her chum was coming back at all. She accepted this morsel of comfort and appeared more cheerful. As for Mary Ellen, the separation was brightened by the picture of a reunion with her family on Far-Side. It seemed so long since she had seen them, and in all that time, no letters—just a few messages sent now and then through the preacher man. Dilly had married and moved away. Little Tom Tad was walking. Her father and the boys had cleared a new ground. Cissie had had the measles. But tomorrow she was going home.

She had a little honeysuckle basket filled with presents for every one of them. Her Christmas presents at the Mission—her Sunday school papers and a few other things. There was an apron for her mother that she had made in the sewing class, and the cutest rag-doll baby that she had made for Tom Tad. Wouldn't he be tickled!

The crowd came early in the afternoon. Men left unfinished furrows, and women left their clothes in the tub to attend the Mission exercises.

First, the children sang their songs and said their recitations, just as they had at Christmas time. Some of the pieces were funny. Little Joe Trotter, who was barely six, took one long breath and recited:

> "My pocket full of rocks
> and my head full of knowledge,
> I'd rather go to this school
> than any other college!"

Of course, the Mission wasn't a college, but little Joe Trotter didn't know it, and it wouldn't have mattered if he had. He had learned that recitation from his Grandpa Trotter who, though seventy-six years of age come next November, had walked up the trail seven miles to hear Joe say the piece which he had taught him.

Mary Ellen had learned "The Bugle Song." Some parts of it puzzled her a little, but she understood something of the beauty in the words. She felt the rhythm of their music.

"Blow, bugle, blow, set the wild echoes flying!"

It made her think of Father's hunting horn far out on the mountain.

She had learned it perfectly, word for word, but when she stood up to say it, she stopped after the first line. A tall form had entered the doorway. It was Abe, her big brother Abe, and bigger and browner than ever. He had his banjo with him, too. Everywhere he went, he took the banjo.

"The splendor falls on castle walls—"

She simply could go no further. The words wouldn't come. Tears filled her eyes. But Miss Ellison came to the rescue.

"There's a vacant seat up in front," she said to Abe, who still stood near the doorway because he saw no place to sit down. And while Abe was coming forward, the next line came into Mary Ellen's head, so she finished her recitation without disgrace and sat down.

"Howdy, Mary Ellen!"

Her heart gave a leap. She had sat down right by her brother!

"Howdy, Abe," she replied. She wanted to ask him questions, but the program wasn't over yet. She must be patient and quiet.

Lovie Lane was saying her piece now. It only had

two verses, and Lovie rattled it off in a hurry and came down to sit by Mary Ellen.

"There's going to be a treat," she whispered. "I saw a box of peppermint candy under the teacher's table."

But something else was to come first. Some folks had caught sight of the banjo and were calling on Abe to "strike up a tune." Everybody on Big Log Mountain had heard that banjo or had heard about it. But Abe was a modest person.

"I didn't happen in to play," he said. "I played last night at a frolic—that's how I come to have the banjo along."

"That's our good luck," laughed somebody.

Abe finally agreed to play a tune called "Sourwood Mountain," and another one called "The Cackling Hen."

Then someone called for a ballad.

Abe pretended he didn't know any, but this was only politeness. After a while, he gave in.

"I might make out," he consented, "to sing 'A Paper of Pins' if somebody will sing the girl's part with me."

There were many girls there who knew the ballad, but they were too shy to say so, and finally Mary Ellen whispered, "Go ahead, Abe. I'll help you sing it."

Abe sang the part of the young man who was courting a fair lady.

> "I'll give to you a paper of pins
> To show you how our love begins,
> If you will marry me, oh, me,
> If you will marry me!"

And Mary Ellen sang:

> "I'll not accept your paper of pins,
> If that's the way our love begins.
> And I'll not marry you, oh, you,
> And I'll not marry you!"

Abe sang:

> "I'll give to you a dress of red,
> Stitched all around with a golden thread,
> If you will marry me, oh, me,
> If you will marry me!"

Mary Ellen replied:

> "I won't accept your dress of red,
> Stitched all around with golden thread."
> She also refused a "dress of green," and a
> "little Tray-dog."

And finally Abe sang the last stanza:

> "I'll give to you the key of my heart,
> That we may lock and never part,
> If you will marry me, oh, me,
> If you will marry me!"

Mary Ellen looked back at the schoolhouse—
a lovely picture to remember.

The fair lady accepted this, and the funny
old ballad ended with a jubilant chord of the
banjo strings.

Everybody applauded, clapping hands so loudly
that, as Granny said, "You couldn't have heard
it thunder."

Then the treat was passed around. Everybody had
a taste of the red-striped peppermint candy. And after
this, Miss Ellison made a little talk and said goodbye
to all the pupils.

Lovie was crying openly now, and Mary Ellen felt
like it, but she wouldn't let herself break down. She
had to comfort Lovie.

As they went up the trail a little later, Mary Ellen
looked back at the schoolhouse. The crowd had gone.
The door was closed, but as she looked, the windows
turned in the late sunlight to gold—a lovely picture
to remember.

THE END

More Books from The Good and the Beautiful Library!

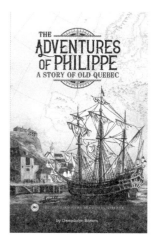

The Adventures of Philippe
by Gwendolyn Bowers

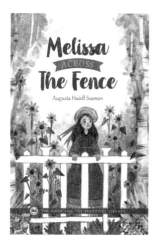

Melissa Across the Fence
by Augusta Huiell Seaman

Juddie
by Florence Whightman
Rowland

Susie and Lizzie
Boxed Set
by May Justus

www.thegoodandthebeautiful.com